I0609802

Perfect

Perfect, Volume 1

Jan Springer

Published by Jan Springer, 2025.

Also by Jan Springer

Club Rendezvous
Shy Girl

Cowboys Online
Her Sexy Cowboys
Her Forever Cowboys
Rescued by Her Cowboys

Cowboys Online Italiano
Tre Cowboy per Natale
Innamorata dei suoi cowboy

Cowboys Online : Moose Ranch
Cowboys for Christmas
Cowboys In Her Pocket
Loving Her Cowboys
Cowboys in Her Heart
Always Her Cowboys

Claiming Her Cowboys

Intimate Secrets
Intimate Lover
Intimate Kisses
Intimate Stranger

Kidnap Fantasies
Jade's Fantasy
Zero To Sexy
Christmas Lovers

Perfect
Perfect

Pleasure Bound
A Hero's Welcome
A Hero Escapes
A Hero Betrayed
A Hero's Kiss
A Hero Wanted
Captive Heroes

Pleasure Bound Boxed Set

Pleasure Bound : COMPLETE SERIES SciFi Erotic Romance Boxed Set

Tentacles Shifter Erotic Romance
Taken by Him

The Desperadoes
The Pleasure Girl
In Her Bed
Awakening Eve
Dark Solar

The Key Club
A Merry Menage Christmas
Sophie's Menage
Jewel's Menage
Jaxie's Menage

The Outlaw Lovers
Jude Outlaw
The Claiming
Colter's Revenge
Tyler's Woman
Resistance
The Outlaw Lovers
Alpha Outlaws Boxed Set

Vampira
Sweet Heat
Dark Heat
Wet Heat
Crimson Heat

Standalone
A Touch of Menage
Shades of Menage Boxed Set
Naughty Girl Desires Boxed Set
Nice Girl Naughty
Sinderella Sexy
The Biker and The Bride
The Fire Within
Bared to Him
Pleasure Bound : A Futuristic Adult Romance Boxed Set
Merry Menage Kisses Boxed Set
Inner Girl Rising
Stripped Naked
Risqué Girl Delights Boxed Set
A Holiday Menage
Ménage À Trois
A Hitman for Hannah
Billionaire Boyfriend
Edible Delights
Vampira
Toygasm
The Dark Side

Watch for more at www.janspringer.com.

Perfect

Perfect Series Book One

Jan Springer

Environmental contamination has made the world unliveable. The sick outnumber the healthy. Hospitals are overwhelmed. Economies collapse. Governments combine to form a one world power called the "Order of Authority"(OA).

To save the human race the OA builds "biospheres"—large bubbles enclosing self sustainable cities. Only the healthy are allowed inside. Everyone else is left to die...For population control, each human is embedded with a microchip, suppressing the urge to mate. The art of lovemaking vanishes...

Centuries later...

A rebel group have tampered with their microchips and begin to experiment with intimacy. Now they search for allies who can help them with their cause – to eventually free mankind.

Recruited to help free humans from a Totalitarian regime, two young doctors seduce gardening expert Anica Maine into a secret world of forbidden pleasure and sizzling sensual experiments.

Perfect Series ~ Book One – Perfect, Book Two - Imperfect

Copyright

Published by Spunky Girl Publishing
Copyright 2015 Jan Springer
Cover Art by Talina Perkins of Bookin' It Designs
Cover photo by Hot Damn Designs
Edited by Julie Naughton & Amelia S. Black

License Note

This book is licensed for your personal use only.

Author Note

This is a work of fiction. Characters, places, settings, and events presented in this book are purely of the author's imagination and bear no resemblance to any actual person, living or dead or to any actual events, places, and/or settings.

Dedication

This series is dedicated to those who believe we are headed toward a dystopian society...that is, if we aren't already there.
The human race is resilient and will always find a way back to their natural impulses. ~ Unknown

Prologue

E arth, 2054
       Environmental contamination has made the world unliveable. The sick outnumber the healthy. Hospitals are overwhelmed. Economies collapse. Governments combine to form a one world power called the "Order of Authority"(OA).

To save the human race the OA builds "biospheres"—large bubbles enclosing self sustainable cities. Only the healthy are allowed inside. Everyone else is left to die...For population control, each human is embedded with a microchip, suppressing the urge to mate. The art of lovemaking vanishes...

Chapter One

arth Year 2304, Biosphere A1Z9

Fear and dread flooded twenty-two-year-old Anica Maine as she uploaded her day's Netmail from her personal compudeck and detected the warning from the Order of Authority.

She swore softly beneath her breath, closed her eyes, and tried hard to still the frantic beat of her heart.

Netmail from the Order of Authority meant only one thing.

It was her turn to be impregnated.

Why she was so surprised was beyond her. All of her friends her age had already headed to the Impregnation Centers, gotten pregnant, had their perfect babies and went on with their lives.

Anica didn't want to bear a child. Not now. Not when her career was in full swing, and she couldn't afford to take time off work.

Besides, she'd heard the stories about how impersonal and boring those impregnation machines were. Some women had to go every day for months before they got impregnated.

Now it was her turn.

Anica sighed heavily and punched in the address to the nearest I Center. It didn't take her long to discover there was a waiting list. A very long waiting list that extended way past her deadline date.

Shit!

A quick scan of all the I Centers in the other Biospheres showed they, too, were booked solid.

It was all her fault. She'd procrastinated too long.

If she couldn't get an appointment, then she would have to go the alternate route of an old-fashioned Doctor.

The Authorities were quickly phasing out those Doctors, now that perfect babies were one hundred percent guaranteed with machines.

But she had little choice.

The law was the law and with so little time left, she was stuck.

"Doctor it is," she mumbled angrily and set about finding one through the compudeck.

"How much do you charge for your baby-making services?"

The soft, sultry voice made Doctor Zack Daly's head snap up from the compudeck screen where he'd been watching the latest illegal sex movie, he'd unloaded off a banned server. He swallowed at the tightness in his throat the instant he recognised the Biosphere's top gardener, Anica Maine.

Damn gorgeous woman. A perfect ten. Six feet tall. Shoulder-length, brown-blonde hair. An hourglass figure. Sparkling brown eyes.

Generous, perfectly shaped breasts pushed up against the tight purple dress she wore.

His cock spasmed the instant his gaze settled on her luscious cupid's-arrow-shaped lips.

Shit! He'd picked the wrong day to unblock his Sex Blocker.

She arched a well-manicured eyebrow. "There was no one at the greeting desk. Did I interrupt you?"

"No! Not at all. I was just doing research." More like keeping himself illegally aroused since business was slow and getting slower.

He shifted uneasily in his chair, maneuvering closer to his desk so she wouldn't notice the hard bulge pressing against his pants. If she got an idea of what he'd been doing, she could easily press charges for him being sexually aroused. He really should be more careful about when and where he disabled his Sex Blocker. With the recent changes regarding the quick phasing out of his specialties in favor of those machines in the

Impregnation Centers, he hadn't really expected any woman to show up today for his services.

Lately, only despairing women with looming deadlines were seeking out his services, and by the way Anica's hands were knotted together she was desperate.

"My baby-making fees are twenty-two thousand super megadollars per hour, which includes my moving in with you until you are pregnant. Or if you prefer, we can schedule your office visits at your convenience."

She frowned, not pleased with his higher fees.

"The Centers only charge nineteen thousand, and a perfect baby is guaranteed," she argued.

"True but going that route, you have a bigger chance of infection from improperly sterilized parts, not to mention the penetrator used is usually too short, unlike myself. With me, you have deeper penetration and a better chance at getting pregnant. Even if the baby is imperfect and terminated, your duty is technically fulfilled, and you can go to court to fight against another impregnation order. I've heard women win those cases all the time."

He could tell by the way her lips tilted faintly at the edges that this would be something she might be interested in. These days, some women would rather work on their careers than do their duty of being impregnated with the recommended one child. It was a loophole the Authority would soon close, no doubt.

"Some women also find that sometimes the machines in those Centers can lose control and do some serious internal damage, thus making it costlier than a Doctor's services. Not to mention the waiting lists in-between impregnation attempts are quite long. Rumor has it the I Centers use all kinds of tricks to keep a woman from getting pregnant too quickly so the Centers can get more money. That's why there's such a long waiting period. By the way when is your deadline?"

"One month from tomorrow."

Zack let out a slow dramatic whistle for effect. "One month. You like to live dangerously, don't you?"

"And you don't?"

She eyed his computer warily.

Shoot! Had she noticed he'd been watching an illegal sex movie?

"You shouldn't smoke that stuff."

"What?"

"The marijuana ad on your computer. You shouldn't even be looking at that. They're talking about making it illegal again. Some people who smoke it too much aren't passing their Perfect Scans and are being eliminated."

"They are?" That was news to him. Maybe he should cut down too.

"I've checked with all the I Centers," she continued coolly. "They have waiting lists longer than one month. If I go with you, how long before we can start?"

Right now, sweetness! I'm primed and ready to have sex with you, perfect lady of my dreams.

"What's your penalty for not being impregnated by the due date?" he asked. Excitement and disbelief shot through him. Anica Maine as his client. Life could not get any better than that.

She shrugged. "I was afraid to look."

"Bring your wrist over here so I can scan your microchip for the information. It's best if we know what we're dealing with. There have been some harsher laws just put in place. If you're lucky, you didn't get nailed."

She held out her wrist. Zack couldn't help but notice the velvety-looking skin of her arm and wondered if the rest of her appeared just as creamy soft. His cock tightened with need at that thought.

Down, boy.

If he played it cool, he'd have this gorgeous gal out of her clothes in no time flat, writhing beneath him, even if she weren't open to being unblocked. But he sensed she would be very sexually receptive in her natural state, then he would do a memory wipe easily enough afterwards.

"Doctor?"

Zack blinked at the interruption. "What?"

"The scan?"

"Oh! Of course. I was just thinking on how best to serve you...regarding your fast-approaching deadline." He lifted his scanner and brushed over the thin microchip that was implanted beneath her wrist.

"The main scanner is busy. It'll just take a moment to break in."

She smiled coolly. "What is your success rate for impregnation?"

"I've a rate of ninety-five percent within a month. Also, a ninety-five percent chance at a perfect baby."

"Could I get a look at your...hardware? So, I can make my decision?"

Shit! He'd forgotten about that part.

Many women preferred to see what they were buying before making the deal. Unfortunately, it was unethical to show a woman an erect cock before a deal was made. She'd notice right away he was illegally aroused.

Think fast, Zack or you're in big trouble.

"Um...yes, of course. I must warn you though my Blocker has gone faulty of late. I've been meaning to get it fixed." Liar, his inner voice screamed. "It's not working today, but I'll let you have a look..."

He forced himself to act casual, as if he walked around with an illegal hard-on every day. Standing, he dropped his pants. With rather shaky fingers he unsnapped the Velcro snaps keeping his cock hostage in the harness.

His hot throbbing dick unfurled quickly, lengthening like a rock-hard iron bar pressing up against his belly. He hadn't realized he was that aroused.

"This is relatively how it will be right before I penetrate you."

He could see a sparkle of fear flash in her eyes as she gazed at the spider web of veins pulsing up and down his thick shaft. The mushroom-shaped head was purple, and it appeared to crave relief.

"It's awfully big. Are you sure it will fit inside me?" She replied calmly. Too calmly.

Her Blocker was in full working order if that was the only question she could come up with. There wasn't even an ounce of curiosity brewing in those gorgeous brown eyes.

"Once I disengage certain sections of your Blocker, your vaginal juices will flow at a greater consistency, allowing for an easier penetration."

Mercy! All this talk was making him hornier. He'd need to engage his Blocker pronto or he'd be wasting his sperm by jerking off in the bathroom.

"May I touch it?"

You touch and I'll explode.

"You touch, you buy," he groaned in a strangled voice.

The slightest tilt of amusement lifted her sensually shaped lips. A more perfect set of cupid-shaped lips there couldn't be in this Biosphere.

The few times he'd experimented with his Blocker and seen her in the Gardens he'd come home with one hell of a hard-on. She would be perfect mating material. Perfect for the experiment he'd volunteered to carry out in his Biosphere after learning about the rebels not too long ago.

Thankfully, she didn't touch him. It was expected. Women weren't sexually aroused with the Blocker in place. There was no need or craving in her to do anything but look.

"When would you be available for the first impregnation attempt?" she asked.

Gotcha!

"Actually, I have an opening right now. A last-minute cancellation. I just called my client and gave her the good news that our last session was a success."

She nodded and appeared nervous.

Uh oh. His cock almost deflated in disappointment at that look. "Is this a bad time for you?" he asked.

"No, I mean...I just didn't expect it to happen this fast."

Zack held his breath for her answer. At the same time, the scanner beeped, allowing him to log her into the database.

Her data popped up on the screen a split second later.

Anica Maine. Perfect ten. Brown eyes. Brown-blonde hair. Twenty-two years old. Never been penetrated.

He read on.

"They got you on the penalty. If you're not impregnated by the due date, they'll come for you and take you to the Penal Biosphere, where they'll keep you on a machine until you become pregnant. That's not a pleasant situation for any woman. I'd advise you to get yourself pregnant fast."

She exhaled softly. "Okay. Let's get started right away."

Fantastic!

Zack tried hard to slow down his harsh breathing.

"You can go straight into Room Number One. It's right through those doors and down the hall. Remove all of your clothing. Put your feet in the stirrups. I'll be there in just a few minutes. I'll download all your information onto my database. I can adjust your Blocker from here, so you'll soon feel your vaginal juices starting to flow. You should notice a change in your body temperature too, once the adjustment is complete, so don't panic."

She nodded and headed towards the door he'd indicated. A moment later, it shut quietly behind her.

Zack closed his eyes and inhaled a deep shuddering breath.

He had Anica fucking Maine in his office!

This was too good an opportunity to pass up. He wanted to bring her into the experiment.

Officially, when he needed to get a woman ready for penetration, he only had to do minor tweaking to the Sex Blocker. Just enough to get her vaginal muscles spasming so she could milk his sperm. The law required the pleasure Block remain intact so the only thing she experienced would be a slight tightening of her vaginal muscles as his cock slid in and out of her. No pleasure created, hence no addiction to sex.

Besides not allowing sexual arousal, the law also dictated that her memory of the penetration be erased afterward.

Zack held an excited breath as he adjusted Anica's Blocker data on his scanner.

Unfortunately for Anica Maine, the sexual experiments the rebels were running weren't following the law.

Chapter Two

Anica couldn't wait to get this impregnation thing over with. What a nuisance to bear a child now that she was finally making a name for herself in this Biosphere. She should have had herself impregnated the instant her menses had started, as most of her friends had done.

They'd had their perfect babies and given them to the Family Unit and gone on with their lives. Now they had their perfect homes and their perfect jobs and were perfectly content.

But no, she had decided early on in life to pursue a career in the Biosphere Gardens. She'd always enjoyed planting things and watching them grow. With her dream job as Head Gardener, her status was also lifted to Higher Woman.

A Higher Woman had more perks, such as more vacations, more variety of rations and more of a choice of where she could live. Unfortunately, she was a woman, and it was her duty to the Biosphere to bear one child.

How in the world was she going to bend over and help with the seedling plants when she was eight or nine months pregnant?

She wasn't a strong woman, she thought as she slipped out of her dress. She preferred the creature comforts of warmth, a belly full of food and a perfect little apartment on the south side. An apartment with a great view that permitted her to see the snow-capped Rocky Mountains through the clear Biosphere bubble.

Now that she had everything in her career, this impregnation thing had come along. She'd been envious of the other women in the Gardens.

Being huge with child hadn't seemed to bother them. They'd taken their duties of bearing the dictated one child in stride.

As Anica slid off her panties, she kept her eyes glued to the bed. It appeared cozy enough, a nice firm mattress with a pale-green sheet covering it. The black metal stirrups with straps looked sterile and were attached to the sides of the bed near the middle. She noted at the head of the bed a couple of black straps with cuffs coming out of the wall.

A shiver of apprehension zipped up her spine. This whole situation seemed surreal, yet it was finally happening to her.

A Doctor telling her to undress so he could fuck a baby into her with that big cock was just unbelievable. Good grief, she should laugh at the irony of this.

When it came right down to it, sex was outlawed. Fucking illegal, except when the woman was allocated her one child.

Sex was considered imperfect. Addictive, a human flaw corrected by the Sex Blocker program included in the microchip embedded in everyone immediately at birth.

Anica sighed and climbed onto the bed.

The mattress was warm against her bare ass as she swung her naked legs onto the bed. She brought her knees up until they almost touched her breasts before she spread her legs wide and slipped her bare feet into the cool metal stirrups.

Oh my! What an odd position to be in.

She watched her bare breasts jiggle sensuously with every inhalation of breath and grimaced at the odd fluttery sensation that unexpectedly slid along her veins.

She'd never noted how wonderfully curved and round her breasts looked. Never realized how large and pink her areoles appeared or how plump and elongated her plum-colored nipples seemed.

Nor had she ever envisioned the Doctor's lips clamping over a nipple and sucking it into his hot mouth.

Anica blinked in shock and forced the carnal idea away. She must be tired. That's why she was thinking such nonsense. She needed to relax and just pretend everything was fine.

Staring up at the white ceiling, she counted the air holes as they blew warm air gently over her splayed-out, naked body.

A strange little knot of something she found appealing embedded itself in the pit of her lower abdomen as his footsteps approached on the other side of the closed door.

The Doctor was coming.

He hesitated on the other side of the door. She could hear his breathing and the rustle of his clothing.

Is he undressing?

Her face flushed with heat.

Would she get another look at that engorged cock before he penetrated her with it?

It had seemed so big and thick and long. The intricate web of veins pulsing along the entire length of his shaft hadn't made her blood boil moments ago as it was doing now. Nor had her vaginal muscles so much as moved when she'd gazed upon the fat, tight sac beneath.

But her pussy muscles were moving quite eagerly now as they clenched in a most interesting way.

She couldn't stop her heart from slamming against her chest as moisture pooled between her thighs. Obviously, he'd scanned the changes into her microchip. This must be what he'd meant about increasing her vaginal juices.

Her breath caught in her throat as the door swung inward and the baby-making Doctor stepped inside.

He wore nothing but the traditional harness, a thin piece of material that bound his shaft and balls tightly against his body keeping his hardware hidden from her eyes. Muscles rippled in his powerful legs as he strolled over to a nearby sink and air sanitized his hands.

"How are you feeling?" he tossed over his shoulder as he scrubbed.

"Fine, Doctor," she lied.

"Please call me Zack."

She nodded.

"I've adjusted your Blocker. You should be feeling your body heating up if you haven't already. In a moment you'll experience other...sensations. Don't let them frighten you. It is a normal part of the adjustment."

His blue eyes twinkled with a strange expression that made her clit pulse as he dried his hands in the air dryer.

She hadn't perceived how tall and handsome he looked when she'd interviewed him. Men were men. No big deal.

But she noticed a lot of new things that had not affected her moments ago.

Thick brown hair curled nicely over his ears and down along his neck. A few brown wisps dangled sweetly over his forehead.

A strange tickle swept over her flesh as she noted his broad shoulders. A thick mat of dark curly chest hair spattered across his well-toned chest. It narrowed and arrowed down his flat belly slipping beneath his harness towards his mammoth bulge. A bulge that seemed a lot bigger than when he'd first entered the room.

His face was shaven as all men were ordered to appear in public, yet she spied the dark stubble of a five o'clock shadow lining his jaw and cheeks. It made him seem like a dangerous yet appealing rebel.

Dangerous.

Alluring.

The strange little knot nestled in the pit of her abdomen blossomed into a feverish heat as he strolled to the foot of the bed and quickly strapped her feet into the stirrups before he gazed down between her widespread legs.

His Adam's apple bobbed wildly as he swallowed and cleared his throat.

"I'll give you a quick examination before we proceed, just to make sure I've made the proper adjustments to the sexual aspect of your Blocker," he said.

She nodded, trying hard not to react to the bizarre warmth his half-lidded eyes caused deep inside her vagina as he stared between her thighs.

No man had ever gazed at her in this way. It was frightening.

And it was exhilarating.

She trembled when he dropped away the end part of the bed and stepped closer, coming in right between her widespread legs.

"I'll just make the bed a little higher so I can get a real good look at you." His heavy breathing made Anica's breasts tighten wonderfully.

A low hum erupted through the room and the bed lifted. It stopped at his chest level.

"A nice internal examination to see how tight you'll be when I insert my cock."

Oh gosh!

She sucked in a breath as his hot fingers grabbed a hold of her plump labia and pulled her swollen folds apart.

"You're creaming very nicely already, Anica," he commented. "Your clitoris is red and puffy."

Anica's eyes widened in surprise as he pressed a finger into her slit. To her horror, her pussy muscles clenched around him.

"Highly aroused. Your hymen is still intact. Very good. It indicates your Blocker works quite well. You are still a virgin and haven't attempted any penetration. And you're so wonderfully tight." His voice was strangled.

His finger massaged the inside walls of her vagina. Another finger slipped against her clitoris rubbing slowly.

"You should be experiencing some...interesting sensations. It's perfectly normal."

She tried to smile. Tried to reassure herself that the tiny erotic explosions nibbling along her clit was what she was supposed to be experiencing. Perfectly normal, he'd said.

In truth, she felt anything but normal. Heated blood flushed her entire body. His scorching touch unraveled her.

Something deep inside her abdomen boiled and her pussy walls clenched eagerly at his probing fingers. Her breasts seemed to swell and harden.

The urge to gyrate her hips made her bite her lip.

What was he doing to her? Why did this feel so...wonderful?

She inhaled another breath, held it, and blew out slowly.

"How are you feeling?"

"Fine," her voice was harsh. Strange to her ears.

He smiled. "I think things are starting to work properly, Anica. You're dripping quite nicely."

She couldn't resist arching her hips closer to him.

"Yes, that's it, Anica. Move your hips for me. Nice and slow."

She did as he instructed finding it no effort at all as her hips swivelled in a physical dance. Dark sensations washed through her like wildfire.

She cried out at the impact.

"Just relax, Anica."

She nodded suddenly feeling very shy as he watched her, an odd stare raging in his eyes.

The sensual rubbing of her sensitive clit built a strange euphoria through her and to her shock a strange mewling moan escaped her mouth.

"Your pussy is creaming so beautifully," he whispered.

His eyes seemed to be glazing over as he worked between her thighs.

Perspiration dotted her forehead. She nervously licked her lips before clenching her teeth and biting back another mewl as his fingers worked their magic and his gaze flicked over her nude body. Her legs trembled.

She swallowed roughly, trying hard not to meet his heated expression.

But she couldn't stop looking at him. Couldn't stop the wicked desire to have him pull out his shaft and just thrust it between her widespread legs.

His fingers slid out of her with a loud sucking sound, and he stopped rubbing her aching hot clitoris.

"We're almost ready, Anica."

Her abdomen tightened magnificently as he walked to the head of the bed. From this viewpoint she caught an angle of his large hairy scrotum bulging out from the sides of his harness as he stood there.

The impulsive urge to lick the sensual outline of his balls almost made her cry out.

"Before we start, we need to get you restrained."

"Restrained?"

"To make sure you remain in the proper position while I'm penetrating you. Lift your arms over your head."

She thought about protesting. Thought about telling him she wouldn't move away from this position.

"It's standard procedure, Anica," he replied in a stern voice.

Why she hesitated, she didn't know. He was a Baby-Making Doctor. She'd given him the right to impregnate her. He knew what he was doing. She had no reason not to do what he told her to do.

She nodded and reluctantly conferred bringing her arms up over her head. She watched with fascinated wonder as her breasts shook and she realized how hard and elongated her nipples appeared.

The cuffs were soft and velvety as he slipped them snugly around her wrists and she noted he smelled good.

Very good.

An inviting scent that made her want to get even closer to him.

With the straps secured around her wrists, he stepped beside the bed and gazed down at her.

His piercing stare raked over her splayed-out body again.

He didn't smile as he spoke. "First, I'll examine your breasts."

Her mind whirled. Examine her breasts?

Muscles bunched in his bare arms as his warm hands cupped her domes. "Beautiful, nice and full and swollen."

He tested their weight, lifting her breasts in his palms. It was a sensual touch she found...arousing.

"Heavy. Very heavy. Like ripe fruit ready to be picked."

As he began a slow massage of one, he cupped the other one and to her shock he bent his head, his hot mouth fastening over her nipple.

Excitement roared as her flesh tightened and swelled. His rough tongue laved her nipple. It tightened as he sucked hungrily, his teeth painfully nipping at her flesh.

Fear zipped along her nerves at the strange, wonderful sensations assaulting her and erupting like a lusty blade of lightning inside her vagina.

Blood pumped into her nipples as his mouth seduced her. Could he feel them distend and tighten into large burning buds?

She was amazed at the wonderful sensations quivering throughout her limbs. A sweet dizziness smothered her.

She arched her back, pressing her hot flesh into his sucking mouth.

A little bit of spittle dribbled out of his mouth as his lips moved expertly, sucking and biting and nipping until Anica wanted to scream from the sweet anguish.

His mouth let her nipple go with a pop and he immediately started in on her other one until it felt just as hot and quivering.

When he finally lifted his head, Anica trembled like a leaf and with half-lidded eyes she watched as he unlatched the straps of his harness.

She inhaled sharply as his giant cock burst loose.

By mercy! He'd grown!

The man's shaft was as big as her wrist, if not bigger. And his length...she shivered involuntarily. She couldn't even garner it in inches. Maybe eight, nine, ten inches long?

What she'd seen earlier in the office had been nothing compared to this.

Her breathing quickened as she noted how those interwoven veins moved as blood poured into his shaft. His cock seemed to grow even bigger right before her eyes.

Fear rippled to a higher notch.

There was no way he could get that monster into her. No way.

Her gaze became transfixed to the mushroom-shaped head that appeared so swollen and deeply purple.

A drop of liquid slipped out of the slit. Tucked beneath his cock was the hairy scrotum, swollen and red and so hard looking.

Her limbs weakened in despair and submission. She wanted him thrusting his cock into her now. Wanted his mouth on her flesh, his hands touching her everywhere.

"Don't be frightened, Anica. You'll enjoy it."

Anica blinked in confusion. Had he just read her mind?

"Enjoy it? I...I thought sexual pleasure was illegal."

"The memory wipe will take care of any guilt or lingering feelings of pleasure."

She calmed momentarily. Everything would be fine. She wouldn't remember this. That was why memory wipes were mandatory. But such pleasure and these unnamed emotions was something she really liked.

He walked to the foot of the bed and stood intimately between her lifted knees.

The bed hummed softly, and it lowered.

"There. I have a perfect aim."

She winced as his finger slid over her puffy clitoris again. He began a slow, torturous massage that had her gasping for breath in seconds.

It felt so wonderful it must be illegal.

"Please, don't do this," she finally cried as the shudders and sensations grew even more pleasing.

"No turning back, Anica. We're in this for the long haul."

Chapter Three

N *o turning back?*
Anica submitted to his words. Or maybe she was weakening with surrender to these wondrous cravings devouring her?

She watched in horrified wonder as he reached over, and he pulled on a knob she hadn't observed before. A drawer slid out of the wall.

From the drawer, he quickly grabbed a small coin-shaped cup. As he took the cup out, she detected a thin red wire attached to it, which led back to the drawer.

"What...what's that?"

"Clitoris stimulator. It'll keep you aroused while I fuck you. It'll fit snugly over your clit."

She'd never heard of a clitoris stimulator.

"Secrets of your trade?" She tried to laugh, to soothe her nervousness but it didn't work.

He didn't smile and she cried out softly as he placed the tiny clear object over her sensitive clit, and it immediately sucked and massaged her swollen wet flesh.

She shuddered.

Heavenly Biosphere! This feels good!

He was absolutely right. The sensual item was doing exactly what his finger had just done, except tenfold as it erotically massaged with expert strokes that had her writhing on the bed.

The device allowed him to free his hand do other naughty things to her.

She couldn't stop herself from crying out as he pulled apart her drenched labia and touched the entrance to her hot pussy with soft sensuous strokes. Her lower belly tightened in an intoxicating manner.

She closed her eyes and continued to swivel her hips in a carnal gesture, enjoying the sultry sensations washing all over her. Her nipples stabbed into the air and her breasts heaved as a sensual fever gripped her.

Something big and hard and hot poked at the entrance to her wet pussy.

Her eyes popped open.

Heart crashing against her chest she gazed down between her quivering breasts and trembling widespread legs and tensed at the sight of one of his big hands holding the root of his stone-hard shaft as he lodged his cock head at her vaginal opening.

"You don't have to watch, Anica," he breathed.

"I...I want to," she whispered staring in utter fascination. This was something she'd never seen before.

Her clit was buried beneath a clear plastic device with a wire leading away into the now-closed drawer. A man's cock was slipping into her tiny slit. Yet it suddenly seemed a perfectly normal thing. At least she believed it for a split second before he threw his hips forward and in one hard powerful thrust his cock shot pain into her.

Anica closed her eyes and screamed out as the intense hurt engulfed her.

Automatically, her feet pushed against the stirrups, struggling to break free of the straps. She pulled at her bound wrists, trying to get away from the searing impalement.

Thankfully, the pain lasted only a few breathless seconds.

He withdrew and powered his thick length slowly into her burning pussy. She whimpered at the soft caress of his solid erection as it slid in and out like hot velvet against her raw vaginal muscles.

"Are you okay?"

She nodded as an odd euphoria engulfed her. Concern etched his features as he watched her intently. Perspiration dotted his brow, and his blue eyes flashed with such a raw heat she gave out a little cry.

"That was your hymen breaking," he murmured through gritted teeth as his sensuous thrusts picked up speed. "Now we begin the impregnation attempt."

Oh my!

His hands let go of the base of his cock and his fingers returned to prey upon her nipples, tweaking her hard flesh until they hurt. But it was a nice hurt. Something she loved.

His rough touch drove her impending passion up another degree. She lay helpless on the bed as he continued to impale her with hard fast thrusts.

She gritted her teeth as the clitoris stimulator sucked harder on her swollen clit increasing the wild pleasure.

Oh! Her vagina needed to be filled so badly.

Her widespread legs shook violently. Her feet remained captive in the stirrups and her bound wrists wouldn't budge an inch as his palms smoothed over her swollen breasts. She writhed against him, and she sunk deeper into the mattress with each of his fierce thrusts.

She was totally at his mercy! It was the most erotic emotion she'd ever experienced in her life.

His rock-hard erection continued to spear into her. Each fierce impalement sinking harder until she supposed he might come right out of her belly. She cried out as waves of something both brutal and beautiful enveloped her.

Her every nerve ending screamed and she couldn't think of anything as she convulsed in ecstasy.

Mercy!

It was so unbelievable! Mind numbing. Body clenching. She could barely breathe, yet she didn't want this obscene pleasure to end.

Her eyes were squeezed so tight she saw stars. Blades of lightning zipped up her vagina and her inner muscles spasmed all around his hot rod.

Grunts of masculine satisfaction shot through the air as his long thick shaft continued to invade her with powerful plunges.

Hot liquid exploded into her, and they both cried out, he with arousal, she in surprise.

Anica's pussy muscles greedily enveloped his cock and milked him. His sperm flooded the inside of her and spilled out of her vagina, dribbling down the crack of her ass.

She hoped his seed wouldn't take hold. She wanted more of this, and she'd pay whatever the cost.

When he withdrew his limp shaft from her still-quivering pussy, she gasped at the sight of her blood on his flesh.

"You can clean up in the bathroom," he said as he bent over and picked up his cock harness giving her quite the eyeful of his rock-hard ass.

She licked her dry lips anxiously. "When...when do we do this...again?"

Oh, please say we'll do this soon!

Without looking at her, he snapped the belt around his waist and lifted the harness over his limp penis and deflated balls, effectively hiding the delicious sight from her hungry view.

"I can meet with you tonight for another session. I doubt you're pregnant on the first try, so I won't even run the test."

Thank you!

She inhaled a shuddering sigh as he leaned over and undid her wrist restraints. Her arms ached as she lifted them and brought them down to clasp over her tender belly. He undid the straps around her ankles, and, to her surprise, he gently helped her lift her feet out of the stirrups.

Grinning down at her, his blue eyes flashed with what she perceived as eagerness. "How do you feel?"

She couldn't stop herself from blushing at his question. "I...good. I'm fine."

Wow! Was she ever fine! An intriguing happiness she'd never experienced before bubbled through her.

"Great. We'll see you tonight then. Like I said, you can clean up in the bathroom and use that exit there. It'll bring you right out onto the esplanade where the air cars are parked."

"Thank you."

He nodded and a warm sensation once again enveloped her as his hungry gaze quickly caressed her breasts then slid over her belly and between her legs.

"It was my pleasure," he replied and then he strolled out of the room leaving her with an unexpected sinking, lost sensation.

He hadn't even mentioned the memory wipe. Hadn't even mentioned readjusting her Blocker back to the way she'd been before.

Had he forgotten? Or would he do it through the scanner or his compudeck? And then she wouldn't remember what had just happened.

A dash of adrenaline zipped through her veins, and she cried out in sudden anguish.

Oh please, no!

She didn't want to forget this experience. Perhaps if she hurried, she could get home and write it all down?

Yes, that's what she'd do. She'd write it down somewhere safe and when the Doctor wiped her memory, she'd know what pleasures she'd gone through.

Lifting herself off the bed, Anica gasped at the soreness between her legs and the bright red spots on the mattress sheet.

Having that Doctor's huge cock plunging in and out of her, his hands roaming over her breasts and the intense sexual arousal...Anica inhaled sharply at the wild tremble of excitement shimmering through her. It all seemed as if she'd experienced some sort of wild hallucination. How else could she explain it?

An arrow of fear gripped her, and she glanced at her wrist, where she knew the microchip was buried just under her skin.

What if the Order of Authority were monitoring her thoughts this instant? Sweet Biosphere!

She hoped she never had to explain what had just happened to her. They'd have her exterminated at merely thinking about sexual arousal.

Anica quickly reined in her anxiety. She was being ridiculous.

She was under the care of a Doctor. He knew what he was doing. She was safe from the OA. It wasn't her fault if he forgot the memory wipe.

Lifting herself off the bed, Anica hurriedly picked up her clothing and shoes and headed to the bathroom.

Chapter Four

"**I** 've brought Anica Maine into our Project." Zack spoke to the dark-haired figure on the terminal screen. He wasn't surprised to see Noah Nicholson frown. His associate knew Anica. Hell, everyone knew her. She'd just been promoted to top gardener in their Biosphere. She would be in charge of creating new foods for everyone's perfect diets.

"Cripes, Zack. We were told not to include any higher-level women in this experiment. The OA keeps an eye on them even more than the lower-level women. You just might have put this project in jeopardy."

Both excitement and dread skipped through him at Noah's warning.

"I want her in. I've already made the adjustments to her Sex Blocker. I think she's well worth the risk."

"So much for keeping a low profile."

"We're supposed to be doing research and bringing in allies to the rebellion. If I kept a low-profile, this project won't get off the ground."

Noah shook his head and leaned in closer to his screen.

"Okay, chill. I'm cool with her. Did you upload the new program you devised into her Blocker?"

"Don't look so worried, my man. The rebels said it's foolproof, undetectable by the OA. They won't notice any changes in her thought patterns or her body-rhythm biofeedback. As far as they're concerned, Anica Maine is going about business as usual. A sexless zombie who loves her work and is at this moment going the route of being naturally inseminated because all the I Centers have too long waiting lists."

"And you made sure you're on birth control?"

"Took the shot before I introduced her to the wonderful world of sex," Zack replied. He tried to keep his voice calm and professional when he talked about her. Protocol with these experiments was to not allow oneself to become emotionally involved. But screw protocol. He'd been aroused every time he saw the natural beauty while he visited the Gardens. He'd never had such intense reactions to the other women he'd encountered. It's why he'd been so surprised and aroused when she'd unexpectedly walked into his office earlier. Secretly, he wanted her like crazy and wanted to get to know so much more about her.

"So? How was she?" Noah asked. Zack noted the interest in his partner's voice and couldn't stop from confessing his feelings.

"She was so innocent and sexy I couldn't get enough of her, and she had a similar reaction. She wants more."

"She showed no indications of freaking out and trying to tell the OA what happened to her in your office?"

Zack shook his head. "I've been reading her thought processes. She's excited yet frightened at both her feelings and about getting caught. She won't try to confide in anyone. If she does, the memory wipe will kick in immediately as protocol dictates, and she won't remember anything that happened or what she was about to confess."

Noah nodded his approval.

"Good." Then he got a faraway gaze in his eyes and spoke again.

"That's what is so wrong with our society. They should lose all the blockers. There's too much control. Things should happen naturally between man and a woman instead of all this bullshit with implanted microchips and sexual pleasure denial. They should make sex legal like the old days."

"I totally agree with you, but that doesn't excuse the illegal stuff we're doing."

"That kind of talk will get you into trouble, my friend. Penal Biosphere or more like Elimination will be our end if they catch us before the rebellion is strong enough to succeed. Besides, any attempt to tell anyone unauthorized to what we're doing, and our memories are automatically wiped by the Rebels. They're keeping a closer eye on us than the OA. Just remember or your out."

"Hey, I'm not backing out. We need to show people how it's supposed to be between men and women."

Noah grinned. "And of course you'll enjoy showing the women."

"This is serious shit." Zack wasn't doing this for his own pleasure. Of course, that was a darned good fringe benefit.

"She was that good?" Noah asked picking up on Zack's earlier excitement.

Zack nodded barely able to contain his enthusiasm as he remembered seeing her nude body splayed out on the table. Hell, she'd been a feast for his hungry eyes and the way her face had scrunched up with such agonizing pleasure when that orgasm had ripped through her, he knew she was more than pleased at her pleasure. Instincts told him that without a blocker, she would grow to be a strong, passionate independent woman.

"Well, since you've already started with her, we'll have to continue with our next appointment and see what happens."

Yes! He could see Anica again!

Although Noah was smiling that cocky grin of his, Zack detected the troubled crease between his eyebrows. Apparently, his friend was still worried about Anica being a Higher Woman.

"When is the next meeting with her?" Noah asked.

"Tonight."

"Are you ready?"

Zack's cock throbbed and hardened at the question. "Very ready."

"Good. I'll see you later."

The secure video feed went dead, and Zack slumped back into his air chair.

Immediately, his thoughts returned to the beautiful Anica who'd been spread out on the table ripe and ready for his taking. Shit! He'd never seen a woman's clitoris so swollen and so purple with arousal. And when he'd seen all that cream oozing from her tiny slit, he'd known for sure she was perfect for their research experiment.

Zack groaned as he recalled how he'd pushed his rigid cock into her tight, wet channel.

Biospheres! The sexy mewls she'd made when he'd impaled her had made him lose his senses. He'd thrust his thick shaft into her so hard and so fast he'd been afraid he might have hurt her, but the rougher he'd fucked her, the more she'd enjoyed it.

She was the perfect one for this experiment. She was the perfect one for him.

Bringing her into the project was a huge risk, but one he was willing to take.

WHEN THE COMPUDECK announced that someone was at her door, Anica didn't think she could answer it.

She still hadn't experienced any memory wipe as was the procedure after an impregnation attempt and ever since she'd left the Baby-Making Doctor's office she'd been a nervous wreck having trouble trying to sort out her emotions. The pleasure she'd experienced beneath Zack's hands had turned her into a writhing ball of carnal lust.

Writing it all down into the secret journal and hiding it on her compudeck had only turned her on even more.

She'd loved the way his huge cock had pistoned into her. Loved the waves of pleasure screaming into her spasming pussy as he'd unleashed his hot seed. Every nerve ending inside her sparkled to life, and she shuddered at the idea that he'd come here to do it to her for a second time.

The compudeck interrupted her thoughts informing her again that Baby-Making Doctor Zack Daly was waiting to enter.

Anica inhaled a shaky breath.

Okay, she could handle this. He hadn't seemed the least bit surprised at the way she'd screamed while he'd impaled her over and over.

What had happened to her must have been a perfectly natural part of the impregnation attempt.

Wasn't it?

But what about the sticky wetness dripping between her thighs? It had been ever present since their last encounter this morning and grew worse as she instructed the compudeck to let him in.

She watched anxiously as the door slid open.

To her horror her vagina clenched, and her nipples stabbed against her thin dress as she spied two men standing there. The Baby-Making Doctor Zack and another man she'd seen around the Biosphere on occasion.

She'd never thought twice about how good-looking the other man was...until now.

The newcomer had short black hair and the darkest brown eyes she'd ever seen. He was way over six feet tall and possessed quite long legs. Both wore the traditional Baby-Making Doctor white garb and carried the black bags.

Anica's heart picked up a frantic pace. Why had he brought this other man here?

"Is something wrong?" she asked shyly.

"Everything is fine, Anica," Zack soothed as he and the other man stepped inside. The hungry way they were both watching her made her nervous. She'd never seen two men look at her like this before. Like she was something to be desired.

Like she was something they wanted to devour.

She inhaled a deep breath to steady the fevered heat rushing through her veins. Her clit swelled and dropped past her pussy lips and a virtual river of cream dripped along the insides of her thighs.

"I've brought along my colleague, Noah," Zack said. "He's also a Baby-Making Doctor. I've conferred with him about your time situation, and we decided with both of us trying to impregnate you, we can make the deadline."

Oh my! Two Baby-Making Doctors?

"Noah has a terrific success rate with perfect babies. He tries unconventional methods that seem to work. With both our sperm sliding into you, you'll be with child in no time flat."

Anica's legs trembled at the idea of two cocks trying to get her pregnant. "Um, can I get you both something to drink?" Heaven only knew *she* needed one.

"No, thanks," Zack answered.

The other Baby-Making Doctor remained silent as he walked over to her couch and opened his black bag.

"We'll get started right away," Zack smiled.

"I'll go into the bedroom and undress."

"Actually, we can do it right here to start. We've discovered that different positions allow for deeper penetration, hence faster fertilization. You may undress now."

"Here?"

Both men smiled.

Anica managed to return their smiles despite her nervousness.

"Everything is fine, Anica," Zack soothed and walked over to her. "I'll undress you and we can get started."

She could barely nod as his fingers went to the hem. Her body was so tight. Her limbs trembled. Her nipples scraped erotically against the material.

"Lift your arms, Anica."

She melted beneath his soft voice and did as he instructed.

The heat of his hands splashed against her ass cheeks as he lifted her dress. Sweet mercy, wherever he touched, a wild fever claimed her.

Peeking over Zack's shoulder she spied the other Doctor watching. His gaze was so dark. Dangerously arousing. She shivered at the sight.

The tips of his lips curled upward ever so slightly.

Her breasts spilled free from her dress and warm air splashed over her shoulders as Zach lifted the material over her head. He dropped it into a silent puddle at her feet.

Both men inhaled sharply as they stared at her nude body.

Her breathing became rougher as she followed Noah's gaze to her breasts.

They heaved up and down with her every breath. Her engorged nipples were elongating, flushing red as blood pumped into them. Anica shifted uneasily at the erotic sight.

"Easy, Anica," Zack whispered.

Anica's breath caught in her lungs as she gazed over at Noah and watched him undress.

"I'm scared," she finally admitted to Zack as fear slithered up her spine. She'd never heard of two Doctors fucking a woman to impregnate her. "This shouldn't be happening."

"We'll take good care of you, Anica. We'll make sure you'll meet your deadline."

"I...I changed my mind. I don't want this."

The wicked sensations spiraled all around her as Noah's gaze darkened. His shirt was off, and she couldn't help but appreciate the sight of all those tense muscles rippling in his tanned shoulders or at the incredible way her tummy tightened as his hands went to the waistline of his pants.

"You don't have a choice in the matter anymore, Anica," Zack whispered in a strangled voice making her turn her attention back to him. His hand smoothed over her bare shoulder in a sensual caress. His palms were so electrical on her flesh.

"We've put in the fucking order," he continued. "The Authorities will come for you if we withdraw it. You don't want to end up on in the Penal Biosphere hooked up to a fucking machine, do you?"

"I'll explain to them I was scared. They'll understand."

They'll have to understand!

Backing away from Zack and the sensual torment has hands were creating, she bumped into a solid wall of heat and muscle. She didn't have to turn to know Noah had circled around. Didn't have to be told that the solid piece of heated flesh pressing against her bare ass was his rigid cock.

"Anica," Noah whispered.

She shivered as his warm breath caressed the back of her neck and his strong hands curled over the curve of her hips. She tried to bolt, but he held her fast.

"Anica, we won't let you go until you're pregnant. That's what you're paying us for. Spread your legs for me, Anica."

She whimpered.

"I won't ask twice, Anica. We're here to do a job, and we'll do it."

She inhaled at the burning outline of his long, hard shaft pulsing against her lower back. The excitement ripping through her was too much to handle. "I...I've made a mistake."

"No mistake. You've just got cold feet due to the unknown. You'll enjoy it. Just as much as we will."

The word "enjoy" rang through her mind. How was that possible? Sexual enjoyment was outlawed. Sex was illegal. How could they do this?

Noah's large hands twisted her around until she stood face to face with him. At the sight of his flushed face and the dark, almost black, eyes, her heart crashed against her chest.

"Don't be frightened. Remember the pleasure Zack brought to you with his cock?"

Oh yes! She nodded.

"Look at my cock, Anica. Look at the pleasure I'm going to bring to you."

She swallowed at the panic surging through her bloodstream and glimpsed down between their naked bodies.

Oh my!

His thick shaft stretched outward from a mat of black curls. Below it she spotted the two swollen egg-shaped spheres full of his baby-making sperm. His penis grew quickly in size; one solid blue vein running up the middle and his entire shaft reddened as blood engorged it.

Wow!

Noah's cock was even longer than Zack's!

And thicker!

Her breath backed up in her lungs at the thought of being impaled by it.

She watched wide-eyed as the foreskin wrinkled and a pink plum-shaped tip emerged from the sheath. A drop of pre cum appeared in the slit.

The sight mesmerized her. Fiery sensations uncoiled through her and she tensed with anticipation.

Was he going to lie her down on the floor and fall between her legs and fuck her the way Zack had done? Was he going to place a clitoris stimulator over her clit and then they would watch her writhe beneath the assault of those wicked sensations?

She needed him to do something, anything to unleash the tension seizing her.

Her breasts were so swollen she swore they would burst. She needed his hands touching her there. Needed his fingers tweaking her nipples until they burned and most of all she wanted him thrusting his large cock into her.

Dizziness swept over her, and she swayed.

Noah's hands tightened like a vise on her hips.

"Place your hands on my waist, Anica."

She did as he instructed, her fingers digging into his heated flesh in order to keep herself anchored.

"You know what to do with your legs."

Oh yes! Her pussy creamed at his words and this time she followed his instruction without hesitation.

To her shock, Noah's warm palms framed her face, and his head descended without warning, his mouth covering hers completely.

Deep sinking sexual awareness churned in her belly as his lips slid over hers in sweet movements. She kissed him back.

His hands dropped from her face, his fingertips brushing along the curve of her slender neck, over her collarbone and onto her breasts. He tweaked and pinched her nipples until they burned, and her breasts became heavy.

She couldn't stop herself from moving closer to him, her hands sliding to the cleft of his strong back, her hips thrusting forward crushing her pubis against his hard shaft. Masculine lips continued to kiss her face, her neck, her shoulders.

His hands left her breasts and slid down her sides. The intense heat of his palms on her flesh made her vagina cream even more and wetness dripped along the insides of her thighs.

Oh!

She longed for his cock to probe between her legs, to enter her throbbing pussy. Craved for him to unleash the magnificent pleasures Zack had given her.

His delicious hands continued downward until he cupped her ass, drawing her ass cheeks so far apart they burned.

To her surprise, a hot cloth pressed like a furnace between her cleft and against the puckered knot of her anus.

"Zack will prepare you down there," Noah whispered.

The glazed appearance of his eyes made a hunger, hot and intimate, rage through her and she couldn't stop herself from mewling like a kitten.

Why down there? She wanted to ask, but her question disintegrated as Noah's hot mouth slid over her lips as he continued to hold her ass cheeks open for Zack.

Chapter Five

Heated blood pumped through her veins as his lips stroked hers, unravelling more illegal pleasure.

She ached. Her ass burned as the cloth intimately rubbed between the curves of her cheeks.

She tried to understand what was happening to her, why they were doing this to her, but in the end, she just went with the carnal sensations enveloping her.

She automatically spread her legs wider as the hot cloth pressed into her tight little hole making her gasp at the erotic sensations. A moment later, it was removed and quickly replaced by a lubed finger, which pushed into her quivering anus.

Her anal muscles clenched around the thick intrusion. The finger moved slowly in and out of her, pushing deeper and deeper like hot lava and then another lubed finger slipped in, unleashing a marvelous pleasure-pain through her ass, making her gasp into Noah's mouth.

Noah's thick tongue was doing wondrous things too, thrusting between her teeth like a miniature cock, following the same plunging rhythm as Zack's fingers in her ass. Her lower belly tightened at the lusty pleasure, and the scent of her sex mingled with the fresh aroma of men.

Breaking the kiss, Noah dropped to his knees before her, his head dipped close to her pussy.

Whatever remnants were left of Anica's fears disintegrated when Noah's fingers parted her nether lips, and his hot mouth seared over her soaked, pulsing clitoris.

Around and around her clit, his eager tongue circled unleashing a dark, wicked joy through her lower belly.

Her legs trembled and Anica thought for sure they would give out. In a flash she curled her hands over his rock-hard shoulders, and she held on tight.

Noah's tongue moved downward, plunging into her steaming vagina. Slurping sounds zipped through the air as he drank her cream.

Zack entered another finger into her ass, filling her with more pleasure-pain. Her mind screamed. She grew taut at the thick intrusion.

Noah's tongue continued to seduce her pussy, burrowing deeper into her wet channel. His tongue was hot and demanding, stroking the walls of her vagina, and pressing against an extra sensitive area about an inch inside.

Her mewls split the air. It was as if she just might lose her mind to the agony of her impending orgasm.

Perspiration popped all over her skin. She thrust her hips into Noah's face.

To her frustration, she couldn't move. Noah's steely grip was still prying her ass cheeks apart, holding her captive for Zack's probing fingers, as he sucked her cream from her.

Anica sobbed when a moment later Zack's fingers left her ass one by one, and Noah pulled his thick tongue out of her drenched channel.

A sense of abandonment claimed her as she stood there. Her eyes were tightly closed. She was feverish with want.

Her asshole throbbed with a need to be filled. Her vagina was on fire, begging to be fucked.

The wicked sensations of frustration overwhelmed her, and she didn't even understand Noah's words when he spoke. He had to repeat himself a couple of times before she understood.

"Anica, can you hear me?"

She sobbed and nodded, tears of sexual aggravation streaming down her face.

She wanted to be fucked so bad she thought she would die if they didn't do her.

"What do you want us to do, Anica?"

"Fuck me." She trembled at the lusty sound of her voice. Shivered at using the forbidden words she'd once read in a recently outlawed history eBook.

"Fuck me hard. Please."

She wanted them so bad, it hurt.

"We'll do her standing up," Zack's strangled voice came from behind her. "I'll take her in the ass. You take her pussy. Let's see how she likes it."

Anica cried out as she stood there and tried to move away when the giant mushroom-shaped head of Zack's thick cock pressed against her trembling anal hole.

"It's too big," she whimpered, fear intermingling with arousal.

"Shh, Anica. I'm here. Zack's lubed his cock and he'll slip it into your ass without too much trouble," Noah soothed into her ear.

His fingers released her burning ass cheeks, and he settled his hands snugly on her waist. "This technique will have your beautiful pussy sucking my seed like there's no tomorrow. Just hold tightly onto me and breathe into it."

Anica's fingers dug deeper into his muscular shoulders.

Her breath caught as Zack's cock sank into her tight hole. Her ring gave way, and he cried out as he pushed inside. Her anal muscles, already aroused by his fingers, clenched around his thick invasion.

Oh, goodness! Pressure unlike anything she'd ever experienced before made her try to move away from him, but Noah's hands kept her firm.

"She's so damn tight," Zack panted.

Anica couldn't stop herself from moaning as his long shaft burned into her. Sweet heavens, she could feel every long inch!

Noah's hot mouth slid over her quivering lips trapping her aroused moans. She tasted her sex on his mouth. A cinnamon-sweet flavor that wasn't unpleasant at all.

From somewhere far away, she could hear Zack's frantic whisper. "I'm almost fully inside her. Just one more inch."

Her pussy watered as Noah's thick plum-shaped cock head forced its way into her wet slit.

Unbelievable thickness powered into her.

Zack's hands slid around her belly, sliding upwards to cup her swollen breasts and he held tight as he plunged his final inch into her.

Pleasure-pain burned into her ass making her grimace.

Noah's hard heated shaft bored into her like a thick piece of hot metal. Her ass muscles continued to clench around Zack as he kept his penis buried inside her. Her muscles blazed and the pleasure had her gasping as Noah's erection filled her vagina to bursting.

She was impaled on both men's cocks. Locked into them. Sandwiched between them anxiously waiting for them to do to her whatever they wanted. What she *craved*.

It made her want to scream at them to hurry. To hurry and make her fly with arousal as Zack had done to her earlier this morning.

Her fingernails dug deeper into Noah's broad shoulders. Every nerve ending inside her was on fire. Her vaginal muscles quivered around Noah's burning flesh. Her asshole blazed with need.

Zack's hands were moving over her breasts, tweaking her nipples. The lower half of Noah's body was pushed into her belly. The firmness of his pubic bones grinding against hers and his swollen balls pressing against her flesh.

Noah stopped kissing her.

"Open your eyes, Anica," Noah instructed.

She did as he asked. His eyes were darker than anything she'd ever seen in her life.

"We're going to fuck you now, Anica. We're going to fuck you so hard, you'll be screaming from your sexual arousal and begging us to never stop."

She gave a little frightened cry at his words. The pleasure-pain from two massive rods burning deep inside her made her wonder how much carnal anguish she might be able to handle.

"Would you like that, Anica?" Zack whispered from behind her, his warm breath caressing the length of her neck. "Would you like to lose yourself in pleasure? Would you like more of what I gave you this morning?"

"Yes," she admitted. She didn't care anymore if this pleasure was illegal. She didn't care about anything except these two men and the wondrous bliss they brought to her.

"I knew you'd like it," Zack whispered, his hands massaging her breasts and toying with her aching nipples. "We're going to start fucking you. If we're lucky, you'll be pregnant by morning."

She nodded shakily.

Noah's smile of approval made her heart pound faster. "Are you ready?"

She nodded.

Their large hands were sliding over her flesh leaving trails of fire in their wake. Her mind spiralled as both slid their hard erections out of her.

She cried out as Zack thrust his rigid cock deep inside her ass in one swift plunge. As he withdrew, Noah's huge shaft plunged into her pussy.

Anica arched against them, not knowing whether to push her ass into the exquisite pleasure-pain Zack created or if she should press into Noah's wild plunges.

Their combined thrusts made Anica explode. She cried out her approval. Orgasm after orgasm ripped her apart. Pleasure consumed her.

Despite her cries of release, the two Baby-Making Doctors continued to pump into her. Fast and furious. Delicious and raw. They used her viciously. Invading her with their rigid shafts.

She writhed and bucked against them, eagerly accepting their heated thrusts. They made her come over and over, made her burn alive and shatter with the carnal pleasure-pain and exquisite joy. Her mind filled with nothing but ecstasy.

Their cocks destroyed her. Made her scream. Made her want more and more.

Perspiration drenched her and sexual exhaustion eventually took hold.

When they finally ejaculated into her, she shuddered at the hot jets of sperm gushing into her spasming channels, filling her insides with blistering-wet fire, her muscles clenching onto their pistons, draining them of their fertile seed.

Her pussy was still trembling, and she gasped for air by the time they withdrew their limp rods.

Weakness enveloped her and strong masculine hands lifted her.

"Put her on the couch. We'll start fucking her there, next."

Oh my!

She couldn't do this anymore. She was exhausted, so weary from their combined fucking.

Warm air pillows cradled her as they lay her down on her couch. Noah's hot lips brushed her kiss-bruised mouth. "You did fine, Anica. Rest."

She nodded and drifted into a sexual slumber.

Chapter Six

Z ack's sperm-filled balls felt as if they weighed a ton as they became engorged once again with his fertile seed. His big cock quivered as streaks of fire curled along his hard length. He was getting harder and tighter by the second just by watching Anica doing what Noah instructed and turning herself over, so she lay belly-down on the couch.

Noah grabbed her by the ankles and pulled her along the silky air pillows until her belly rested on the edge of the couch. He moved between her widespread legs and Zack slipped in behind Noah, holding tight to Anica's ankles.

Peeking around Noah's broad shoulders he got a great view of her pussy and what he observed made his cock harden even more.

Good man! Look at the way her cream is seeping from her slit.

"I'm going to penetrate you again, Anica. But this time in your ass," Noah warned her.

She glanced over her sensually shaped naked shoulder and Zack noted the fear in her eyes.

It was most likely fear, because she knew Noah's cock was a hell of a lot bigger than his, and he hadn't taken her in the ass yet. He'd seen the same look in the other woman they'd done this to.

Double penetration had been a part of their bosses' research protocol. They had to examine how a woman reacted with two cocks plunging inside her.

While they'd fucked Anica, all her reactions had been recorded via the scanner inside Noah's black bag. It read her brain waves, fluctuating hormone levels, level of sexual arousal, her thoughts, everything. It was all scanned back to the Rebels so they could see exactly what was happening here.

There was no doubt they would want Anica in the fold.

Zack's heart quickened as he gazed at her breasts. Enormously swollen, they pressed seductively against the air pillows. Her curvy ass was ripe and ready beneath Noah's palms as he played with her plump cheeks.

She whimpered as Zack spread her legs wider.

"Why in the ass? Why by yourself?" she whispered.

Zack grinned. She wanted both of them again.

"Because it'll arouse you in a different way. It'll make you want us even more," came Noah's soft reply.

But Zack knew the truth. Double penetration had ruined her for a single man. From now on she would crave two, or even more, men to fuck her.

Anica cried out her arousal and Zack couldn't stop from moaning as with one big thrust Noah's entire ten-inch-long penis disappeared into her ass.

By gosh! Zack had been right about her. She was the perfect woman for their sexual experiments.

THEY TOOK ANICA OVER and over. Sometimes she fought them. Fought the arousal that their hot touches created. Fought the strong hands that held her down while the Baby-Making Doctors took their turns fucking her.

The stretching, the fiery pleasure as each one penetrated her either vaginally or anally, had her screaming out for more, just like Noah had said she would. She had endless orgasms. They had endless erections and ejaculations.

Endless lust. Sometimes she didn't fight, opting to give herself over freely to the illegal pleasure from their seducing mouths and their hard cocks.

They took her in all positions possible. Her legs thrown over Noah's shoulders, while Zack held her body in the air, and Noah's solid shaft impaled her. They took her while she was on her hands and knees. One cock filling her mouth, the other fucking her pussy.

She convulsed. Jerked.

Her vagina creamed over and over again making it so easy for them to penetrate her on a continuous basis.

She begged them to double penetrate her.

They didn't, telling her they knew better. Telling her that single penetrations would make her next time with two men even better. But how could it ever be better than what she'd experienced most of this night?

Finally, in the wee hours of dawn, the two men carried her satiated nude body to her bed. They lay on either side of her, their satisfied snores ripping through the air.

When her compudeck's voice prodded her awake, informing her it was time to go to work, Anica groaned her protest. She wished she didn't have to go to work today. The mere idea of both men waking up and taking her, of thrusting their hard cocks into her aching pussy and sore ass in such perfect unison, made her want to scream.

Maybe they would agree to move in over the next month? Maybe they would fuck her 24/7? She could arrange the time off. She was due some vacation time. But first she needed to get ready for work. If she didn't show up, they'd scan her room and find out the real reason she hadn't come in. They'd scan her memory and discover all the obscene pleasure she'd experienced.

Oh, sweet heavens, she couldn't let that happen.

She'd leave the Baby-Making Doctors a note, that's what she'd do. She'd tell them she wanted them both trying to impregnate her and they could move in tonight.

Truly, she couldn't afford to hire two Baby Making Doctors, but she'd beg, borrow, and steal for more of this awesome sexual experience.

Strolling into the bathroom, Anica noted the pregnancy test scanner on the counter. During a fucking intermission, Zack had explained how to use it. All she had to do was scan her wrist a few minutes after awakening. Her microchip would record if she were pregnant or not.

She thought about not doing it, pretending she'd forgotten. But, again, a quick scan of her memory would reveal her lie, and being deceitful was highly frowned upon in the Biospheres.

Following the instructions Zack had given her, she then took a quick air shower. Minutes later, as she tried to figure out what she should wear to work today, she pondered on perhaps purchasing a new dress? Make herself pretty for the two men for tonight's session.

Anica froze.

Look pretty for Baby-Making Doctors?

No, she couldn't do that. They'd think she was experiencing too much pleasure. They might readjust her Blocker earlier than needed. She knew the sexual pleasures she'd experienced during these fucking episodes would be erased from her mind when she got pregnant.

Hopefully, when that happened, she would be able to find the written experiences buried in her compudeck and she could somehow relive this again.

Goodness, how could she go back to life without sexual pleasure? The mere thought of it made her breath back up in her lungs in sheer terror. She'd never felt so alive as when Zack and Noah were fucking her.

But there was no way out of going back to life as being a virtual sexless zombie.

No way in hell.

"OH LOOK!" ANICA'S BEST friend, Michaela, screeched at the twenty-foot bio-feed screen of today's live news as Anica entered the locker room after putting in a hard day's work in the Gardens.

Anica rolled her eyes and stifled a chuckle as her friend's shoulder length tangled cocoa brown colored hair bounced around as she shook her head.

Michaela was always overreacting to the live news. Sometimes Anica wanted to put in a request with the Authorities to ask them to adjust her excitement level to a lower degree. But then Michaela wouldn't be Michaela anymore if she did that.

When she spotted her, her friend's green eyes sparkled with wild excitement.

"They're talking about Baby-Making Doctors in Biosphere K9X2," she squealed.

Anica focused on the bio-feed scan and tensed as two unfamiliar Doctors were being handcuffed in an office-like setting that looked a lot like Zack's office.

Her whole body went cold, and she almost cried out her shock as she listened to the commentator.

"Tampering with Blockers to unacceptable arousal levels were upon making a woman become addicted to sex," rang in her ears.

"Can you believe that?" Michaela cooed from beside her. "Doctors stooping so low as to allow a woman to experience sexual pleasure while impregnating them?"

No!

She barely heard Michaela as she spoke. "The commentator said the best-case scenario for those Doctors would most likely be chemical castration and a life sentence in the Penal Biosphere. The Order of the Authority wants any woman who has been exposed to those kinds of Doctors to turn themselves in for readjustment. They think there may be more of those Doctors out there. Ha, I doubt there will be any readjusting going on. They'll be eliminated along with any unborn. It's just a ploy to get the women to turn themselves in.

The Authority can't guarantee that the Doctors haven't implanted some sort of untraceable virus or other hidden program in the Blocker that will keep them addicted to sexual pleasure."

Virus? Terminate? Anica's head swam. Was that what was happening to her? Dr. Noah and Dr. Zack were getting her addicted to sex so they could arouse themselves using her?

"The OA have confiscated the Doctors' records and will track down all the women under their care," the commentator's monotone voice droned.

What should she do? Throw herself at the mercy of the Authorities, and tell them she believed the same thing might be happening to her? They would understand she was a victim, wouldn't they? Besides, other than her experiencing pleasure at the hands of two men she was deemed perfect. Her health was perfect. She'd dedicated her life to doing a perfect job. Now that she was a Higher Woman, they wouldn't kill her so easily.

Would they?

"Are you all right, Anica? You look pale." Concern etched Michaela's pretty features.

"I'm fine. Must have been something I ate." She tried to keep her emotions under control. despite her need to scream hysterically. Tried to maintain a calm voice despite the wild tremor ripping through her throat. She couldn't afford to create any suspicions.

Michaela was her best friend, but she, like everyone in the Biospheres, was programmed to turn in a criminal immediately, no matter if she was a friend or not.

Even if Michaela went against her training and decided to help her, one quick scan of her friend's memory would reveal to the OA that she'd helped her, and Michaela would be eliminated. She couldn't do that to her dear friend.

"I was experimenting with a new breed of what I had hoped would be the perfect tomato. I don't think it'll agree with our stomachs. The acid level is still too high."

Her friend laughed. "I told you! But do you listen to me? The seedless variety just doesn't seem to be perfect." Having said that, she returned her attention to the bio-feed.

That's when Anica slipped out of the locker room. Her heart crashed against her chest as she left the building and headed for her air car. Once inside, she breathed a sigh of relief.

If the Authorities had discovered she was experiencing sexual arousal at the hands of Noah and Zack, they would have put a blocker on her air car and come to arrest her by now. She was safe.

At least for now.

Programming her vehicle to take her home, her mind whirled with what she should do as she flew past the hundred-floor skyscrapers silhouetted against the clear bubble of the Biosphere that kept everyone alive and perfectly healthy.

First, she needed to get rid of any evidence that the Doctors might have left behind in her home. Then she needed to get them to give her a memory wipe. Then she'd be safe from elimination.

Shoot! How had she let them use her so easily? She'd known all this pleasure had to be illegal. If she didn't get a wipe, there was no way she could avoid getting caught.

Anica sighed.

Goodness! What should she do? Truly she didn't wish to return to a life without such exquisite pleasure. But it was the only way to stay alive.

Her air car beeped ripping her from her thoughts. She was home.

A moment later the air car secured itself to her two-hundredth-floor apartment door. The hatch opened and she entered her cushy apartment.

Panic assailed and she wiped away the tears of frustration.

"You've heard the news."

Anica trembled as Zack's voice sailed over her jittery nerves. Whirling around, she saw him standing in the bedroom doorway. Despite her confusing emotions, she couldn't stop the flash of excitement at seeing him wearing nothing but a cock harness.

He stepped forward, his eyes flashing a hot lusty stare that speared anger straight through her. Reaching out, she slapped him across his face. The sharp sound and raw sting of flesh hitting flesh made both of them cry out.

Shock flashed in his eyes and Anica gasped at the red handprint erupting across his right cheek.

"You're trying to get me addicted to sex so you can pleasure yourself," she accused. She didn't care that Noah now stood in the bedroom doorway. Didn't care that he studied her reaction with curiosity examining her as if she were some sort of bug in a biology experiment.

Her anger burned brighter as she focused her fury on Noah. "And you too! You should both be ashamed of yourselves. What you are doing goes against the Order. If I didn't fear elimination, I would turn you both in! As it is, I'm sure they've read my thoughts and are on their way as we speak."

"Easy, Anica. We can explain the truth," Zack replied as he reached out trying to take her hands into his. She slapped his hands away. They'd brought her too much pleasure. How could they bring her so much pleasure? How could they do this to her?

Tears streamed down her face. She was sobbing. Crying in despair at what she was about to demand of them.

"You..."

Sweet Biosphere! She had to tell them.

"You have to give me a memory wipe. I don't want to be eliminated. This is illegal pleasure. I want nothing to do with it."

Liar! She wanted everything to do with it. The arousal felt so good. Unlike anything she'd ever experienced before. It was so beautiful. How could the OA deny everyone this pleasure?

Sweet Biosphere! She was already questioning how things were. They would surely kill her when they found out.

"Anica, we're part of a rebellion in the making." Noah's words were spoken with care and tenderness as if she were in a fragile state and would snap and start hitting him as she'd hit Zack. It took her a good moment to realize what he'd just said. When it registered inside her brain, it was as if an explosion had just gone off. Her heart began pounding and her breath became erratic.

"A...a rebellion?"

"A group who wish to release everyone from a life of control."

Zack spoke. He smiled at her, as if trying to worm his way out of getting hit again. Despite her need of wanting to slap both men, she tightened her fists in an effort to control herself.

"People need to be controlled," she snapped. "Or we'll end up extinct, like it almost happened in history. You should know that. We've all been taught what happened in the past. We've all been told why we need to be controlled. We were naturally addicted to gambling, money, smoking, sex, and fossil fuels, and that's just to mention a few vices. We were imperfect back then. We are perfect now. We're alive because of the control."

Noah broke in, his eyes flashing and his nostrils flaring. He seemed determined and angry now.

"You sound like one of those endless reels of memory discs they make us listen to while we slept as children, Anica. It's called brainwashing."

Brainwashing? A technique used in the Penal Biosphere via a person's Blocker to correct a delinquent behavior. Children were not brainwashed. They were innocent. Just untrained in control. They had no right to compare the two.

"You're insane. I don't wish to hear this. I want you to give me a memory wipe and then leave. I don't want to hear anymore of this nonsense."

She trembled. Shaking with a fear she had never known before. It couldn't be possible that life without order would thrive. Yet even as she thought it wasn't possible, she hoped that it could happen.

"What you're experiencing now are your true emotions, Anica. Curiosity, denial, confusion, and guilt to name a few. Like yourself others have gone through this. Most have accepted the new way they feel."

"Others? There are others you've done this too?" To her irritation the idea that Zack and Noah had been with other women seemed distasteful to her. She wanted them both for her and her alone.

Selfish? Definitely!

Zack continued.

"There have been several women under our care. They have been placed with other males to continue the experiments. The two of us have only recently been approached by the rebels. We've begun their sexual experiments and recording our emotions associated with finding out how the OA has kept us emotionally, physically, and spiritually controlled. We've also come to the conclusion that many females do not wish their male or males to pleasure other females."

Her mouth dropped open in surprise. How interesting. Other women felt the same as she did?

Noah chimed in. "The experiments, that is if you choose to continue, will be between the three of us. We've put decoy programs in place in the video feed to your apartment as well as your Blocker in order to avoid detection of what is truly going on. But there is a low chance the Order may get wind of this."

Noah's eyes were blazing as he carefully watched her for a reaction. She forced herself to keep her face impassive despite the curiosity slicing through her. Exactly what kind of experiments did they wish to partake? More of the exquisite pleasure she'd experienced last night?

"If we are caught," Zack continued, "we could get as easy as the Penal Biosphere or as hard as extermination. We'll leave it up to you if you wish to continue with the sexual experiments. Just realize, if you try to utter a word of what has happened between the three of us, anything about the rebellion or anything that may compromise the rebels, the Blocker has been instructed to initiate an immediate memory wipe from just before you met me. You'll not remember me or Noah or what happened. Do you have any questions?"

Questions? Her mind whirled with them, and she couldn't seem to grasp one thought out of the many that bombarded her.

"I need some time to think," she confessed. *And lots of time to figure out what to do.*

"We can give you only a couple of hours," Noah answered. "But we'll need an answer tonight. Just know that we, both of us, truly want you to continue in these sexual experiments with us. What we learn from each other will be recorded and compiled with the information other members are supplying the rebels."

"When is this rebellion?" she asked, as curiosity took a firm hold. It felt liberating to know the OA couldn't read her thoughts. Oddly enough she believed Zack and Noah when they told her the chances of them getting caught was low.

"There is no set date. It's too early in the experimental phase to theorize what would happen if everyone's Blockers abruptly stopped working," Zack explained. "As you can feel yourself, things are confusing right now for you. You can imagine the chaos if everyone suddenly began following their natural urges."

Anica nodded as a picture of what had happened to her first with Zack, and then with Zack and Noah, flipped through her head. And what she'd experienced had been controlled.

Zack sat on the edge of her air couch, the sight of his cock harness making her breath hitch as he studied her with a lust-filled gaze.

"And just so you know, Anica. The memory wipe applies to everyone who joins the rebels, including Noah and myself. All three of us are in it together. From beginning to end, if you choose to continue."

Interestingly enough, that revealed fact made her feel much better. Made her feel as if she wasn't the only one being targeted. As if she wasn't the only one untrustworthy. But she could understand why the rebels wanted to protect themselves. She'd heard that life in the Penal Biosphere was no picnic for someone deemed with a fixable flaw in their personality or a physical imperfection they could overcome such as being overweight.

Hmm, perhaps investigating life without control could be a worthy cause, despite her initial doubts.

Zack stood and joined Noah near the bedroom doorway.

"Any more questions?" Noah asked, his gaze pinning her like a needle into a butterfly.

Nothing that couldn't be answered at a later time, she mused. She shook her head.

"We'll wait in your bedroom for your answer. But just so you know, you aren't pregnant. We both used injected protection and will keep using it until it becomes necessary to impregnate you to fulfil your obligation to the Biosphere. If you ask for the memory wipe, then you'll have to begin a new search for a Doctor or an I Center."

Both men moved to enter her bedroom.

"I've made my decision," Anica replied in a rush. Hope flashed in both men's eyes as they turned around to face her.

Sweet Biosphere! She had to be mentally deficient to have come to a decision so quickly. The last thing she wanted was to find another Doctor or an I Center or not remember Zack and Noah and the exquisite pleasures they brought to her.

She certainly did not wish for the OA to control her emotions anymore. She wanted more sex. More pleasure.

She wished to explore more of these interesting emotions she experienced when both men gazed upon her naked body with such bold stares that made her feel intense heat within her.

Both of them were watching her as she slipped off her dress. As the light cloth puddled at her feet, she knew she wouldn't have to verbally give them her answer. Her body would do all the talking for her.

The End

More from Jan Springer ~ Erotic Romance

Here are some more Jan Springer stories.
Imperfect
(Perfect Series #2)
Jan Springer

ENVIRONMENTAL CONTAMINATION has made the world unliveable. The sick outnumber the healthy. Hospitals are overwhelmed. Economies collapse. Governments combine to form a one world power called the "Order of Authority"(OA).

To save the human race the OA builds "biospheres"—large bubbles enclosing self sustainable cities. Only the healthy are allowed inside. Everyone else is left to die...For population control, each human is embedded with a microchip, suppressing the urge to mate. The art of lovemaking vanishes...

Centuries later...

After learning her friend, Anica Maine is involved in illegal intimate experiments, Michaela Long is thrust into her own naughty world of forbidden pleasure.

Doctors Flynn Campbell and Bryce Davids are immediately attracted to the cute young brunette assigned to them and swiftly introduce Michaela to incredible pleasure with their scorching ménages. Easily addicted, Michaela is determined to keep her newfound enjoyment and her men a secret, even if it means facing Elimination if she is caught.

Alpha Outlaws Boxed Set (Books 1-5 Outlaw Lovers)
5 Books!!

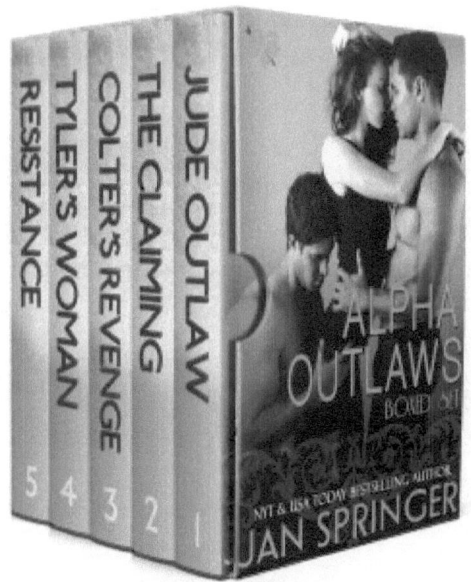

In a world gone mad...
A fast-acting virus has killed a majority of the world's female population. With the creation of The Claiming Law, groups of men suddenly have the right to claim a female as their sensual property and the sexy Outlaw

---

1. https://janspringerauthor.files.wordpress.com/2010/07/alphaoutlaws_js_box_final.jpg

brothers are going to declare ownership of the women, they love...any way they can.

Jude Outlaw

When Cate Callahan learns Jude is coming home from the Terrorist Wars and is ready to claim her under the new law—with the help of his four brothers—she steals their boat and escapes to the high seas.

Unfortunately, her runaway bid for freedom doesn't last long. Quickly capturing his lover, Jude rekindles the flames and seduces Cate back into his bed.

But Jude holds a secret that could make him lose Cate forever...

PLUS

The Claiming

Seeking refuge from the Claiming Law, Callie Callahan hides in a deserted cabin in the Maine woods and is shocked when her ex-flame finds her. She's always craved being in Luke Outlaw's arms. Tasting him. Touching him. Taking him deeply within her. So, what's a girl to do but to delve into the sinful delights he offers.

Luke has finally reunited with the love of his life. He knows there is only one way to keep Callie safe and with him forever. He'll do it with the help of his three brothers and an assortment of naughty toys.

Rekindling the flames between them, he unleashes Callie's sensual side, taking her in ways she never dreamed possible, all with the ultimate goal of introducing her to the Outlaw Lovers and The Claiming.

Colter's Revenge

Revenge belongs to Dr. Colter Outlaw when he unexpectedly reunites with the beautiful woman who broke his heart during the Terrorist Wars. Capturing her, collaring her, and holding her against her will, he seduces her, fills her with wicked desires and naughty cravings for a delicious ménage. Fully intent on breaking her heart and walking away, Colter's plans unravel when he submits to the carnal pleasures Ashley gives him so freely.

Colter had told her he loved her. He'd whispered promises of rescue from her life as a slave, but when he'd suddenly disappeared, she'd been devastated. Infected with a version of the X-virus that leaves Ashley Blakely sexually excited on a daily basis, she has come to Pleasure Palace to bid on a cure for her illness. She never expected her Outlaw Lover to be there and screw her plans. Nor did she expect to give him her heart and body so easily...

Tyler's Woman

For years Tyler Outlaw and his best friend, Hunter Brown, endured brutal torture and worse in an overseas terrorist prison. Finally, free of their hell, they return home intent on seducing Laurie into their erotic-filled fantasies.

Laurie Callahan has always experienced red-hot pleasure and passionate love in Tyler Outlaw's arms. But when he's pronounced MIA, presumed dead in the Terrorist Wars, Laurie's world is shattered, and her heart is broken.

Shocked to discover Tyler is alive and he's taken a male lover, Laurie is thrust into a sensual world of sizzling seductions, scorching ménages, and the carnal desires that both scarred men crave. But she fears Tyler won't want her when he discovers she's not the same woman he left behind...

****READER CAUTION IS ADVISED (m/m forced scenes) ****

Resistance

In the near future, a virus has been unleashed, killing a majority of the world's female population, forcing the introduction of the Claiming Law. A law that states men have all the rights and women are sexual property claimable by groups of men.

Fugitive female...

Renegade Resistance leader Reena "Red" Wilde is in for the fight of her life when she experiences an erotic attraction to the two most dangerous men she's ever met.

Black ops assassin...

Months ago, Will "Blade" Smith spent one sizzling evening in the arms of a red-haired seductress. Now she's his next assignment. One look into her gorgeous eyes and he's wrestling his heated cravings for her all over again.

Bounty Hunter...

When Cade Outlaw nabs his bounty, sexy-as-sin Reena Wilde, his profession dictates she's hands-off. But he can't ignore the magnetic sparks between them...or that she is the biggest temptation of his life.

Resistance is futile...

After Reena escapes Cade and Will and falls prey to a band of evil hunters, she's grateful her sexy hunks come to her rescue...and in return, saves their lives. Trapped in a solitary cabin during a wicked snowstorm, she can't resist her two, well-hung studs, nor can she deny they've claimed her heart.

T

Pleasure Bound Boxed Set Books 1-6

Jan Springer

THIS COMPLETE SCI-FI fantasy erotic romance series contains SIX
BOOKS.

Journey into romance, bondage, abduction, adventure, alien love,
ménage scenes and more.

During a top-secret mission to explore a newly discovered planet
the Hero siblings are thrust into a sensual world of intimate fantasies,
pleasure-pain, violence, unconventional romance and sizzling sex.

A HERO'S WELCOME - 1

Being shot and held captive isn't what astronaut Joe Hero had in
mind when he agreed to a top-secret mission to explore a newly
discovered planet for NASA.

But a man would have to be dead not to fall for the sensual female
doctor in charge of his care.

A HERO ESCAPES - 2

Queen Jacey has always fantasized about bedding a male.

But taking one for her enjoyment is strictly forbidden. That is, until an attractive well-hung stranger from another planet makes her overcome her training and her beliefs.

A HERO BETRAYED - 3

Astronaut Buck Hero didn't count on being held captive or becoming infected with passion poison when he agreed to explore a newly discovered planet for NASA.

If he doesn't get the cure soon, he's going to be one *very* dead man. What's the cure? A twenty-four-hour sex marathon with a woman.

A HERO'S KISS - 4

During a secret NASA mission to locate their brothers on the faraway planet of Paradise, the Hero sisters become separated after they crash land...and find unexpected romance with the tormented male warriors of the newly discovered planet.

Jarod and Piper

Being injured and infected by sensuous swamp water isn't what Piper Hero signed up for when she agreed to search for her three missing brothers. But when she's rescued by a dangerously sexy man who makes her so hot that she can't even think straight, Piper is glad that she came.

A HERO WANTED - 5

(loosely connected with this series)

Old-fashioned gal needs a man who loves to walk in the rain. Must be well-hung. A homebody, white picket fence-type of guy. Sexual requirements-gentle yet untamed lover. He must be sexually adventurous who will train me to be same. Must be romantic, enjoy toys, interested in mutual light bondage, ménages are welcome.

That's what full-figured, antiques shop owner Jenna MacLean wants when she and her best friend outline a want ad just for fun on their weekly girls' night out.

After years of being away from his pretty-plus sized ex-girlfriend, Sully's back in town. When he finds the want ad, he knows he's the only man who can make all of Jenna's sizzling-hot fantasies come true.

CAPTIVE HEROES - 6

Jan Springer

During a secret NASA mission to locate their brothers on the faraway planet of Paradise, the Hero sisters become separated after they crash land...and find unexpected romance with the tormented alien male warriors of the species in this ultra-long sci-fi book.

Taylor and Kayla

While searching for her brothers, Kayla Hero is bound and imprisoned by the Breeders— along with a male captive whose tantalizing scars pique her interest. Forced to escape with him, she's irresistibly aroused when she suddenly becomes *his* captive.

Blackie and Kinley

Injured and lost in a dense jungle, Kinley Hero is intimidated by the scarred man who hunts her, especially due to the power of erotic submission he holds over her.

These stories were previously published by Ellora's Cave.

Cowboys For Christmas
Cowboys Online 1 ~ Moose Ranch #1
Jan Springer
A Canadian Contemporary Ménage Romance m/f/m/m Series

Jennifer Jane (JJ) Watson has spent the past ten Christmases in a
maximum-security prison.
The last thing she expects is to get early parole, along with a job on a
remote Canadian cattle ranch serving Christmas holiday dinners to
three of the sexiest cowboys she's ever met!

Rafe, Brady, and Dan thought they were getting a couple of male ex-cons to help out around their secluded ranch, but instead they get an attractive and very appealing female.

In the snowbound wilds of Northern Ontario, female companionship is rare.

It's a good thing the three men like to share...

They're dominating, sexy-as-sin and they fill JJ with the hottest ménage fantasies she's ever had. Suddenly she's craving cowboys for Christmas and wishing for something she knows she can never have...a happily ever after.

Other stories in the Cowboys Online Series (m/f/m/m)

Cowboys In Her Pocket, Loving Her Cowboys, Cowboys in Her Heart, Always Her Cowboys, Her Forever Cowboys, Claiming Her Cowboys, Rescued by Her Cowboys.

More stories by Jan Springer at http://www.janspringer.com

Jasmine Black ~ Erotica

(a.k.a. Jan Springer writing as Jasmine Black)
Here are some Jasmine Black stories.

Taken by Two Prison Guards
Twenty-three-year-old Madeline "Mad" Madison has quite the temper.
She got ten to life in prison due to her getting mad at her late boyfriend
and there's only one naughty way she knows of to keep herself calm and
she's not getting *that* type of rehabilitation in prison. That is, until she's
assigned hard labor on a chain gang and is taken by two prison guards.

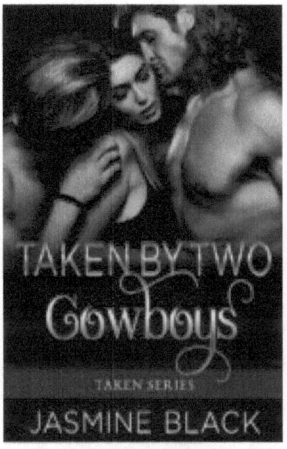

Taken by Two Cowboys

Sierra Allan works hard at her late-father's horse ranch. When her
stepbrother adds her handy girl services to a private auction to help raise
money for the failing ranch, she figures there's no harm...but she's
stunned when her services are sold to two sexy cowboys who give her an
erotic way to save the ranch—submitting to their dark desires...

Taken by Three Billionaires

Billionaire friends, Liam, Theo, and Elijah have just won Princess Isabella in a billionaire card game. Isabella knows exactly what the three men will want from her...she just hadn't expected to have all three of them at once!

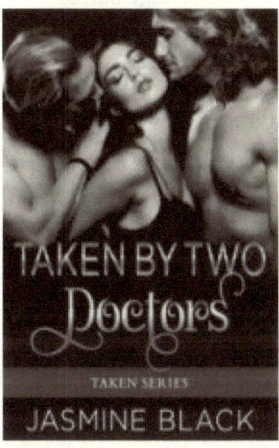

Taken by Two Doctors
A BDSM Medical Fetish Erotica Quickie MFM

Waitress Jean Spelling visits her controversial doctor once a month for some much needed...stress relief. She looks forward to putting her feet up in the stirrups and enjoys Dr. Ball's naughty unconventional treatments. This time when she arrives, she's surprised to discover that she'll be physically examined by two doctors, and they'll prescribe her some much-needed release right there on the examination table! More stories by Jasmine Black at http://www.jasmine-black.com

Ménage series
Taken by Three Bodyguards
Taken by Three Bikers
Taken by Three Billionaires
Taken by Three Doctors
Taken by Three Cowboys
Taken by Three Prison Guards

Taken series.
Taken by Two X-Husbands
Taken by Two Sugar Daddies
Taken by Two Prison Guards
Taken by Two Elves
Taken by Two Mountain Men
Taken by Two Cops
Taken by Two Santas
Taken by Two Lifeguards
Taken by Two Firefighters
Taken by Two Bikers
Taken by Two Billionaires
Taken by Two Bosses
Taken by Two Cowboys
Taken by Two Personal Trainers
Taken by Two Carpenters

Jasmine Black Website ~ http://www.jasmine-black.com
Twitter ~ @blackerotica1

Here are ways we can connect:
Jasmine Black Website at http://janspringerauthor.wordpress.com/
jasmine-black/
Jan Springer Website at http://www.janspringer.com[1]
Instagram – http://www.instagram.com/janspringerauthor
Facebook - https://www.facebook.com/janspringereroticromance
Pinterest - http://www.pinterest.com/janspringer1/
Jan's Blog - http://janspringerauthor.wordpress.com/blog-2/
Happy Reading,
Jasmine Black / Jan Springer

---

1. http://www.janspringer.com/

Don't miss out!

Visit the website below and you can sign up to receive emails whenever Jan Springer publishes a new book. There's no charge and no obligation.

https://books2read.com/r/B-A-WGQ-YDXDG

BOOKS 2 READ

Connecting independent readers to independent writers.

www.ingramcontent.com/pod-product-compliance
Lightning Source LLC
Chambersburg PA
CBHW051932240626
47153CB00004B/1458